The Gracie Series

Praises for The Gracie Series

"The stories are fun to read. They are funny!" ~Aaliyah, 5th Grader

"The stories are engaging and thought-provoking!" ~D. Cain, Grandmother of 9

"The series is perfect for teaching sequencing to emerging and primary readers."
~L. Moots, Elementary Teacher

"The books are engaging, excited to get to the end!" ~C. Bonness, Retired Teacher

"Gracie is a very determined little girl!" ~A. Miller, Elementary School Social Worker

About The Gracie Series

The Gracie Series, written and illustrated by Grace LaJoy Henderson, follows the lovable character Gracie as she gets caught up in funny situations. Parents, teachers and librarians will enjoy sharing these engaging stories and listening as the children share their thoughts sparked by the discussion questions in the back of each book.

The Gracie Series consists of six books: *Popcorn Behind the Bush, Cake in My Shoe, Water in His Face, Math on the Table, I Trimmed My Edges, and Puppy Ate My Shorts!* Each story was inspired by entertaining memories from the author's own life, hence the name Gracie; teaching valuable life lessons while inspiring young readers to use reason, analyze and think critically.

Your child will love these heart-warming stories and so will you!

Each book in the series is sold separately at Amazon.com
Available in Kindle eBook, soft cover, and hard cover
Ask for it in book stores and libraries
Published by Inspirations by Grace LaJoy
www.gracelajoy.com

Popcorn Behind the Bush
Copyright 2017. Grace LaJoy Henderson
Written and Illustrated by Grace LaJoy Henderson
Published by Inspirations by Grace LaJoy
Raymore, MO 64083

ISBN: 978-0-9987117-1-3

Printed in the United States of America

The Gracie Series

Popcorn Behind the Bush

Grace LaJoy Henderson, Ph.D.

Popcorn

Inspirations
by Grace LaJoy

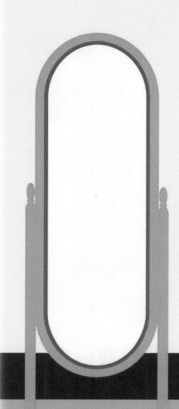

It was a cold winter morning. Gracie was sitting up in her bed under her warm and cozy blanket. She was feeling excited because it was Saturday and school was out for the weekend.

Suddenly, the telephone rang.
Gracie ran into the other room
and picked up the phone.
"Hello?" said Gracie.

It was Grandma! "I am calling to see if the mailman delivered the large tin of popcorn I sent you," said Grandma. "He should have delivered it to you yesterday."

Gracie was surprised. "No," she replied. "I have not received it." So, Grandma told Gracie to look on the front porch to see if the mailman left it there.

Gracie said goodbye to Grandma, walked quickly into the living room and pulled open the front door. She did not see the popcorn. But, she discovered a note stuck on the front door, which read: "Popcorn Delivered – Bush." Gracie was puzzled. She did not understand why the mailman wrote the word "bush" on the note.

With the note in her hand, Gracie hurried into the kitchen where her mother was preparing a healthy breakfast for the family. Gracie told her mother about the popcorn that Grandma sent and asked her if she knew why the mailman wrote the word "bush" on the note.

"Oh my!" said Mother. "Maybe there is a *bush* in our mailbox!"

"No, I don't think so," said Gracie.

Gracie rushed to the dining room where her father was reading the newspaper and drinking coffee. She told her father about the popcorn that Grandma sent and asked him if he knew why the mailman wrote the word "bush" on the note.

"Oh no!" said Father. "Maybe there is popcorn growing all over a bush in our yard!"

"No, I don't think so," said Gracie.

Finally, Gracie walked into the family room where her brother was playing a game on his electronic tablet. She told him about the popcorn that Grandma sent and asked him if he knew why the mailman wrote the word "bush" on the note.

"Wow!" said Brother. "Maybe the mailman is standing on a bush in our yard, eating popcorn!"

"No, I don't think so," said Gracie.

Gracie walked away feeling sad. Then, she looked at the note one last time.

Suddenly, Gracie remembered the large bush in front of the house and began to smile. "I got it!" she said with excitement. "Bush!" Gracie walked swiftly to her bedroom to put on her warm winter coat, hat and scarf. Then she slipped into her snow boots.

She darted towards the front door, opened it quickly, went out into the front yard, and looked carefully behind a large bush. There, on the white snowy ground sat a large tin of popcorn safely tucked behind the bush!

The End

What do you think?

1. Who sent popcorn to Gracie?

2. Where is the *first* place Gracie looked for the popcorn?

3. Who is the *first* person Gracie showed the note to?

4. Why did Mother think the mailman wrote "bush" on the note?

5. Who is the *second* person Gracie showed the note to?

6. Why did Father think the mailman wrote "bush" on the note?

7. Who is the *third* person Gracie showed the note to?

8. Why did Brother think the mailman wrote "bush" on the note?

9. Where did Gracie *finally* find the popcorn?

The Gracie Series

Collect them all!

About the Author

Grace LaJoy Henderson has earned a PhD in Christian Counseling with an emphasis in Writing and Research. Her graduate degrees are in the fields of Education, and Curriculum and Instruction. Her undergraduate degree is in Social Psychology. She has served youth in public school, church and community settings. She enjoys talking, reading stories and sharing poetry with youth and adult groups.